Trail
Blazers

D0582604

Books are to be returned on or before
the last date below.

10/08

Rans⚬m

Trailblazers

Speed
by David Orme
Educational consultant: Helen Bird

Illustrated by Demitri Nezis

Published by Ransom Publishing Ltd.
51 Southgate Street, Winchester, Hants. SO23 9EH
www.ransom.co.uk

ISBN   978 184167 647 0

First published in 2008

Speed

Contents

Speed

Get the facts

How fast can you go?

Before 1829	Getting around is slow. You could: ✔ **walk** (about **3 – 4** miles an hour), ✔ travel on a **stage coach** (average speed of **7** miles an hour), or ✔ ride a **horse**. A horse can gallop at about **25 – 30** m.p.h., but soon has to stop for a rest!
1829	The **Rocket** – travelled at **30** m.p.h. with thirty passengers.
1890	The first cars – **10** m.p.h.
1902	Fastest car reaches **76** m.p.h.
1904	First train and first car to reach **100** m.p.h.
1912	First aircraft reaches **100** m.p.h.
1938	Fastest ever steam train – **126** miles an hour.

1945	First jet plane to reach **600** m.p.h.
1976	Concorde flies passengers at **1,350** m.p.h.
1990	Fastest train – **320** m.p.h.
1991	The Space Shuttle flies at **17,000** m.p.h.

Impossible speed barriers

30 M.P.H.

REDUCE SPEED NOW

Early train passengers thought that it would be impossible to breathe if you travelled at more than this speed!

THE SOUND BARRIER

REDUCE SPEED NOW

Sound travels at around **760 miles an hour**. People thought it was impossible to go faster, as aircraft would break up or be impossible to control.

THE LIGHT BARRIER

Light travels at **670,616,629.384 miles per hour** (*phew!*). Scientists say it is impossible to travel faster than light.

But where have we heard that before?

Going fast on land

For centuries the fastest way to travel was by **horse**.

The fastest Roman messengers could travel **200 miles** in a day.

Early **stage coaches** like this were very slow. It would have taken **10 days** to go from **London** to **Edinburgh**.

During the 1840s, **railways** were built around the world. By 1850 the top speed for a train was **78 m.p.h!**

The fastest way a passenger can travel on land is still by train. The **Eurostar** from London to Paris has a top speed of **190 m.p.h.**

The Japanese **Bullet Train** travels at **220 m.p.h.**

Thrust SSC – just the thing to get you to work on time?

The fastest speed on land is by a **rocket powered car**, Thrust SSC. In 1997 this car broke through the sound barrier and reached **763 m.p.h.**

Most countries have **speed limits** on their roads. In the U.K. it is 70 m.p.h. **Speed cameras** photograph drivers who go too fast.

It's watching you ...

Because of **congestion**, road journeys are taking longer. The average speed in **central London** is **10 m.p.h.**!

Going fast on water

It isn't easy to go fast on water.

This is a Roman Trireme.
It had 170 rowers.
At top speed, it could
move at . . .

8 M.P.H!

This is the Cutty
Sark. It was built in
the 1860s and was
one the fastest ships
of its time.

The usual time to
travel from China to
Britain was 120
days. The Cutty Sark
did it in 90 days –
that's an average
speed of . . .

14 M.P.H!

In the nineteenth century thousands
of convicts were taken to Australia from Britain.
The journey took around six months, and many
of the convicts died on the way.

This is the World's fastest ocean liner, the SS United States, built in 1952.

The SS United States today – a bit sad.

The United States could cross the Atlantic in under 3 and a half days at speeds of up to . . .

40 M.P.H!

The fastest ever boat is the Spirit of Australia. In 1978 it raced across the water at . . .

317 M.P.H!

At this speed, it could cross the Atlantic in nine and a half hours!

...t least two people have been killed trying to beat this record.

Going fast in the air

Early planes

Aircraft have to go fast. Heavy aircraft like passenger jets have to go very fast or they will stall and fall out of the air.

This is the **first ever flight**. The top speed was about 10 miles an hour!

The first really successful passenger planes were **flying boats**. They landed on water.

During the 1930s, you could fly from Australia to Britain in one of these. It took 10 days. It stopped to take on fuel up to 32 times.

You had to be very rich to buy a ticket!

Jet aircraft

Jet aircraft were invented during the Second World War.

In 1947 an aircraft cracked the **sound barrier** for the first time, travelling at 760 miles an hour.

Now the flying time between Britain and Australia is about 23 hours. A non-stop flight would take about 20 hours.

Concorde was the world's first – and maybe last – **supersonic plane**, travelling at 1,350 m.p.h. This is twice the speed of sound! It could fly from London to New York in about three and a half hours. It last flew in 2003.

The world's fastest manned plane is the NASA X-43A scramjet. In 2004 it flew at nearly 7,000 m.p.h!

At this speed, it could travel from Australia to Britain in an hour and a half!

Going fast in space

Why do rockets need to take off so quickly?

A rocket fired into space needs to fight the force of gravity. To do this, a rocket needs to be travelling at about seven miles a second.

That's 25,000 miles an hour!

The space shuttle can travel in space at 17,000 m.p.h. It is easy to travel in space where there is no air.

The problem comes during landing!

The shuttle enters the atmosphere on the opposite side of the world to where it is going to land.

The pilot steers an S-shaped course, using the air to slow the shuttle down. The air friction makes the shuttle very hot. The landing takes just under an hour.

Space passengers

Some very rich
people have
already paid for a flight
to the international space station.

Soon there will be regular trips into space.

You can book your ticket for a Virgin galactic flight
now! Go to www.virgingalactic.com.

Trip to Mars?

Scientists are
planning a mission
to Mars for as early
as 2015.

It will take at least
 to get there.

This
is how long it took
convicts to get to Australia
in the nineteenth
century!

Going . . . really slowly!

The **fastest** thing is the **speed of light** - 670,616,629.384 miles per hour.

What is the slowest thing in the world?

A snail?

A snail can rush along at **0.03 miles per hour**! (At this speed, it could get from Britain to Australia in about 40 years!)

A fingernail growing?

Fingernails can grow a whole **millimetre in a week** – as long as you don't keep biting them! (Toenails grow more slowly.)

A mountain rising?

Mount Everest is rising at about **10 millimetres a year** – a lot slower than your fingernail, but still not as slow as ...

a stalactite?

This can take more than 100 years to grow 10 millimetres.

SO WHAT IS THE SLOWEST THING IN THE WORLD, THEN?

It's a **clock**, and it hasn't been built yet.

The clock will tick just once a year. The **century hand** will move once every hundred years.

The clock will **chime** (or a cuckoo will come out) **once every thousand years**. The clock will keep time for at least 10,000 years.

It's called **The Clock of the Long Now**.

This is the first go at building one – a **prototype**. It is in the Science Museum in London.

17

All
About
Speed

Chapter 1:
"I passed!"

"Guess what! I passed!"

Simon was over the moon. He had passed his driving test just before his eighteenth birthday. Simon's dad was thrilled too.

"Brilliant, Simon! I knew you would do it! Now, any ideas for a birthday present you'd like?"

"A car of my own?"

"No chance! But what about that rally driving experience you were talking about? We could afford that!"

Simon had found out about it on the Internet. A day driving a rally car – skids, handbrake turns, high speed driving through the forest – great!

There were six people on the rally course that day. Simon's instructor was a guy called Tom.

The first part was boring. They all sat and watched a safety video. Then it got better. They all practised handbrake turns on a rough bit of ground. That wasn't part of the driving test!

The instructor showed Simon how to do handbrake turns …

Chapter 2:
"This is rally driving!"

There was a lot to learn.

"Forget what your driving teacher taught you," said Tom. "This is rally driving, not going to get the shopping!"

Once they had the handbrake turn sorted, they learnt about power slides and car control driving on gravel. Sometimes they used the brakes and the accelerator at the same time!

When the instructors were sure the students could handle the cars, they let them take turns to drive round a short course. A guy called Ben had the fastest time. Simon was second.

After lunch, they tried the forest track.

Tom drove first, to show how it was done. It was a really scary ride, though Simon tried not to look scared as they slid sideways past trees at eighty miles an hour.

"This is the tricky bit," Tom said. "It's a steep slope down to the river. Watch!

"Steer with your brakes and brake with your steering wheel! And keep your nose up when you hit the water!"

Chapter 3:
The most brilliant thing

The car started to slide down the track.

Cleverly, Tom flicked the steering wheel and gently used his brakes so the car slithered down at an angle.

Simon thought he would slow down when he got to the water. But he didn't. He pressed the accelerator!

The car splashed through the shallow water and out the other side. The run was over.

It was the most brilliant thing Simon had ever done.

"O.K.," Tom said. "Now you know how to do it. Take a break while I take one of the others round. Then you're in the driving seat!"

Chapter 4:
Not all about speed

Ben had driven the forest track first, and had set a great time. Could Simon beat it?

"Remember what I said," Tom said. "It's not all about speed. The way to get a good time is to be in complete control of the car."

The first section went well. Soon they were at the top of the hill. Just the slope down to the river.

They started down. Too fast. Simon turned the wheel to the left. Then he pushed the brake pedal down.

Nothing happened.

"No brakes!" Simon yelled.

He pumped the pedal up and down. Nothing.

"Gears! Change down now!" Tom yelled.

The gear box squealed, but the lever went in. But then Simon turned the wheel too much. The car slid round. Simon felt the wheels lifting.

The car hit the water sideways. By a miracle, it didn't turn over.

"Well, that's one way of stopping," said Tom calmly. "Fancy another go in a different car?"

"You bet!"

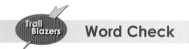
Speed word check

accelerator

Atlantic

atmosphere

Concorde

congestion

convict

Eurostar

flying boat

friction

gallop

gravity

handbrake

light barrier

liner

MAGLEV

manned

messenger

mission

m.p.h. - miles per hour.
Ten miles per hour
is roughly the
same as 16
kilometres per hour.

passenger

power slide

prototype

rally driving

scientist

scramjet

sound barrier

space shuttle

stage coach

stalactite

supersonic

Trireme